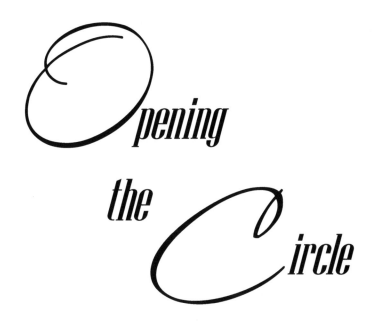

MARY MARCHES

Order this book online at www.trafford.com
or email orders@trafford.com

Most Trafford titles are also available at major online book retailers.

Print information available on the last page.

ISBN: 978-1-4907-9612-3 (sc)
ISBN: 978-1-4907-9610-9 (hc)
ISBN: 978-1-4907-9611-6 (e)

Library of Congress Control Number: 2019909607

Trafford rev. 07/11/2019

www.trafford.com
North America & international
toll-free: 1 888 232 4444 (USA & Canada)
fax: 812 355 4082

Contents

*B*ook Summary

This book is called Opening the Circle for the reason that in these pages I have tried to open readers to reach beyond what might be their ordinarily closed circles of friends, relatives, and every day types of knowledge. I have tried to intensify rather than normalize thoughts, feelings, and beliefs. I have done this hoping that I might not only expand my own horizons, but also to spark the innovative spirit in us all. Isn't it new ideas that are the life's blood of invention and curiosity?

In the interest of encouraging space exploration and alien contact that may have occurred on earth long ago I have written various fantasy poems about extra-terrestrials and strange sometimes illogical alien planets. I have explored the illogical also for the reason that I thought about people before photographs were invented who would never have believed that television was possible!

I have greatly enjoyed reaching for abstract metaphors and similes because it made me feel fresh, new and alive. I have always believed that readers were amused with this sort of expression.

As you will see for yourself if you read this stirring book, I have expressed strong emotional convictions about war and peace, and also some strong ties to religious concepts. Some of my nature poems were inspired by such phenomenon.

I have written in several different styles usually including rhyme and verse perhaps because of my own exposure to these various influences. I did not feel that I could adequately express everything intended within just one style.

There is a lot of the use of colors here. In fact I have written few poems without the use of at least one color word.

Other things you will see a lot of are trees and moons perhaps because these seemed to be full of mystery and romance to me. I hope you will be benefited by the romance of life I myself so devotedly believe in throughout all of its various phases.

I could not of course leave the children out of my book because they are the ultimate embodiment of innocence and all that is really cute and funny in life. What would our world's romance be without their adorable face but a very boring moon that did not give her light?

Author Biography

I use the pen name Mary Marches rather than my legal name and full identity description for the reason that I live humbly in the public view and must try to retain my privacy and safety to wander free and easy. I do not wish to be pestered with questions and romantic attractions about my literature, nor do I wish to provide lessons for the perusal of younger writers. As to the latter, I must apologize that I am a bit under educated to feel like an authority on how to develop writing skills. I want you to know that I am not affluent. I just live on S.S.I. and don't even drive a car due to my disabilities, so that all of this poses a problem about personal exposure. I don't want my family questioned either. They all tend to be very private citizens.

I was born in Spokane Washington, and though the family moved from there when I was too young to remember it, I am told that the autumn leaves are spectacular there! I know I must have been influenced by them because I have retained an inspiration about it that seems mystical to me. I remember hearing the song, "The autumn leaves drift by my window, the autumn leaves of red and gold." I have pictured myself being born in a pile of leaves though I know I was born in a hospital.

My mother and father lived during world war two, and I have not realized until my old age that I completely failed to ask them about their experiences. I was overwhelmed when I learned about the wars in high school and did not like studying history. I thought there was not a perspective given on all of world events, what to remember as permanent knowledge from what could be transitory. I still feel that way, but the reason I don't have many college credits is mostly because of my disability.

I used drugs in the 70's including L.S.D. but don't recommend that you try it! It contributed to insanity more than creativity. I was creative from an early age and was encouraged to pursue my talent legally and safely. I am also an artist of painting, drawing, sculpture, and song and encourage all people to dabble a little. Its therapeutic!

Opening the Circle

Young ladies rock themselves to sleep in chairs
As if no breeze gave life to the white root.
Only the thin mist tells us that lost fear is softer
Than that great abyss by a mountain.
Gray pelicans remind us the river of logic is floating
As we dream of our beds and our rice and black hair.
The peaks are pins at the base of our skulls.
We all look at each other from civilization
But our mouths are wilder than freedom,
Mouths that are now open to the greatest darkness.

Nothing would be worse than forgiveness, not so.
Its pink-gray wind leans back opening the circle
With those Chinese ladies tied on the tongue
The love of hearts and dragonflies has won.
They are like a cloud radius in the great circle,
Their number three point one four one five nine
Sewing the torn slips of pink subtle bodies
Washed out of danger by the old Tao masters
Who got drunk and stared at the abyss with their ears.

Sad masters fear the zero in the number line may add
All of negative and positive matter into an endless void,
The great black mountain no longer for our feet
And the Mayan calendar really twenty thousand twelve
Marking the dead line lest we be restricted to our hell.
In this Zen emblem the three looks like a pyramid
In a cube with lightning that strikes the top
Where the small tip of this five pointed star folds down,
Looking like Scarborough Fair with its mystical doors

Made to push optical illusions into the fifth dimension.
There the particles of the great predators are absent
Since the scarab of Egypt resists poverty near death,
And all that has troubled us must bring us rest.

For those who revered love the mercy cloud grew,
And karmic inertia was to float upward instead of down
To the surfaces of planets with tropical green clowns.
Our Jesus in the lovely lily was gently ascended to
With its yellow radius covered with dew.
His pallid forehead told the story so we cried
That the tears of Filbert could never be mended by a lie.
He was a master whose thoughts were stilled and tied
To paradise with the waxing and waning of the moon
That looked like red and green rings of eclipse
With colorful vegetable ribbons tied through the center.

The Planet Amends

My friend is a spotted leaf of black and white
That is named the elephant plant for such ears,
Soft velvet joined to a blind massive body,
Each one with its trunk like the stamen of a lily
That has grown thick and gray, the intellect of years
With its pollen of stars, the emotions of night
Gathered by a body that hums with second sight.
Purple legs wrapped around it as the bumble bee lotus
Is this soul's meditation on the beauty of the sun,
And its body is a black moon that defies description
In a sky that is green having soaked up new life
Of the morning dew that comes up from the ground
Making a strange sort of elephant sound
Which permeates everything, and so my good friend
Is the leaf of a singing medicine named Amends.
The top side is white with black spots quite sudden,
And the underside is black with white spots so dear
That they resemble the soft belly of an animal
Who nursed her young with attentive ears.
She listened to the sound of this bright red forest
Where musical people and their riddles feared to see
Blank rabbits in the meadow where my elephant plants grew
Casual popcorn and other things that I knew
Like rainbow lobes of a brain or wet pulse pushing memory
On the planet Amends with a purple sun above the city.

Haunted Face

Love's sweet melody held in his soft eyes
Lucid with the wet language of night;
A nose mounting the precipice of philosophy
And lips red with the wisdoms of eternity.
There were two wisdoms, one blessed from above,
And the other pouted resembling a dead dove.
Black hair wrapped his face as if it were my own.
His ears were the patience of obedience.
Nonsense Nonsense was his name.
He stood by an old brick school building
Where ivy climbed the ribs of a round window
He leaned out of and threw me a lonely rose.
His red soul held more than I could ever know.
Smooth muscles left my senses for a dim moment
When the full moon eclipsed this haunted face;
A stranger I thought I once saw on the stage,
Who seemed to want me to silently mimic.
Romantic knowledge danced in his nimble hands.
The long fingers being arrows of various colors
Studied a strong clean jaw like a wooden bow.
Then his eyes closed like the fingers on a flute
Heavy with the haunting of purple ebony.
His red soul held more than I could ever know.

The Planet Iron

Green rust tasted sweet to the fishes of Iron.
They were vegetarian swimmers with molten joints,
Their hard bodies never decaying, eternal life
For as long as their planet orbited night,
A strange black sun of that zenith in heat
With a passion too animal to be incomplete.
The weird furry atmosphere above Iron's oceans
Was always damp with a silent devotion
Massaging these waters with its spongy winds
To make them relax above the sand and its sins.
The sand insects kept a little food chain to eat
Those less evolved species that were microscopic
And made the sand insects develop an itch
That they never stopped scratching till they scratched off rust
That came from the kelp trees that were thick and painless
With their beautiful shining leaves of copper
Growing up from the deep mud of unknown otter.
Otter was a living metal with millions of eyes
At the core of this planet keeping it mesmerized,
But only the unknown otter really ate nothing.
So much nothing was missing from the planet's core
That it caused a slow rotation of the seasons of doors,
Making confused Iron fishes taste the golden nobs.

$\mathcal{S}$ponge Night

Old God is as innocent as a bucket of pink paint,
Thick and smooth and pretty in His puritan form,
Always resilient as a sweet backward essence
My cobalt might mix with casting rainy shades
Of violet or purple which simmer this haze
Of cloud potatoes or storm animals that won't die,
Poking out intoxicated from their spiritual eyes.
As His soft sinking sun turned inside out in the sky,
Mixing wild red into this paint makes it excite
Sparkling roots of sexuality that are feral white
Except for their pastel rainbows that are the skin.
This animal skin must build up a thick gray or sponge night,
In its depth parted, exposing a wrinkled pink eraser.
Many have tried tanning the lobes of listening brains
With a trembling teacher who pencils in no subject
Except for strong ones that stuff fat rainbows
Or cows who drink pink paint for immortality,
Like my sponge night when it soaks up utter existence
Then squeezes out the remains as an old yellow bucket.
Yellow is the thick hardening of war's inferior,
An interior holding paint for the bridges men fear.
Grassy spiritual bridges are fastened with God's tears
Like spongy green nails of sentiment finding bliss
Irresistible to my sponge night in the indigo spirit
Hiding an African violet as God's pink yet unborn.

The Abnormal Child

A pretty little extra-terrestrial with red hair like the robe
That sleeping Jesus wore almost down to his toes
Had accordion fingers wrinkled and somewhat funny.
Oleander was her name and Limbo was her bunny.
She was dressed up in lace by a nurse who played her mother.
We told her the stars were fathers and that space was her brother.
Oleander put on black tights she was old enough to wear,
And she told her mother Violet that she loved to share.
This funny little girl wrote poetry and told Oristalana
She could read when she was three and slept out in the sauna.
She rode a horse when she was four who she named Timbanana,
But what this redhead loved the most was polka dot pajamas.
Oleander had a delusion that freckles were little bugs,
And insisted on going out at night all wrapped in purple rugs.
Her eyes were glowing indigo thought of as quite frightening,
But a scientist said they were as normal as thunder and lightning.
She was only a normal child on her planet called Simmer,
But on Earth, although smarter, she was never the winner.
Oleander was quite psychic so she always knew the answers,
Accused of cheating by her black teacher who was a dancer.
One cloudy day they came from Simmer and must take her,
Leaving only red star dust in an Oleander salt shaker.

A Symphony at Midnight

Midnight Violet was a symphony rarely imagined.
Suspicions couldn't write it. We've been too weak to dream
Of the inside of music so very sentimental
We were saturated by the beauty of its theme.
A philosophy inside of Africa, the wet bamboo flute
Always playing in harmony light hearted and sweet;
Yet woodwinds at odds with the strings had clashed
With a dissonance for a moment that tasted like beef
To shy children who were frightened by the tuba solo
That kept stumbling about the dull confusions of death,
Until tenderly she took back her deep violet breath.
This flower then faded until stuck in the moon
Imbedded in her cave where my echo snaked,
And all sounded like the triumph of many harmonies
Which grew dim and flat and suddenly slaked.
Purple wings of a butterfly soon drank their fill
Of the green meditation she left in my will
Suspended as this black body with its dangling legs;
A symphony at midnight, the stem of starvation.

Black Fish

The little black fish in my heart
The little black fish in my heart
The little black fish in my heart
A secret of sorrow.

Pink violet melts into sea
Pink violet melts into sea
Pink violet melts into sea
Blue trace of tomorrow.

Gray seagulls grow dim on the shore
Gray seagulls grow dim on the shore
Gray seagulls grow dim on the shore
Like black sand on arrows.

When sad Jimred hunted with bow
When sad Jimred hunted with bow
When sad Jimred hunted with bow
He pierced a black sparrow.

Ridiculous waves of the night
Ridiculous waves of the night
Ridiculous waves of the night
Ninth logic of marrow.

Pajama Eyes

Soft stretchy aliens with pajama eyes
Plotted to stop the pollution of cries
By putting heavy lids on cloud bumps
Until these sad aliens all caught the mumps.
They looked like balloons blown up and cinched,
And their drawstrings were all wet wimps
With little space ship ends, hot knots
Kids parents could not understand but bought
Because stars all seemed like knots meant to gloat,
So it was cool to be limp and hairless the most.
Then you might draw worship as a ghost with taste
On your cross as an intersection in space
Where you take on fuel from planet noses below,
And your smile whispers things parents never know,
About how pajama eyes stick out like columbines
Curving forward to read the Alien Times.

Tweed Walls

Concerned for our planet and the cries of our race,
We mourned reincarnation with its breath of many lives
As a man who lost one and said no more of wives.
Like winter trees that resembled black shoes,
Blue wind passed right from the day through the night
Until it was picked up by beauty and pulled tight
In threads of tweed that wrapped around every color.
But the tweed master was sensitive, stroking our bumps
With his I.Q. of eight hundred to turn red to gray.
His gray kneaded eraser was stuck everywhere
By the time he pushed green bumps all out of our cares.
We feared then to touch them, those tweed walls of space,
And thanked the strange master although it was not
The first winter coat that was worn by our cops.

The Visitation

The crown of many thoughts appeared in my tree,
A complex of twigs and thick branches of emotion
Supported by a trunk of hollow genius that defined
That weird bark of wisdom I might collect
A piece of to write my poetry of intrepid nonsense on.
I wrote long sentences about the empathy of synapse
Being frustrated by the crucifixion of details
With little moments tucked in before the appearance
Of light was found superior to a benign darkness.
We sat still in this holy night and tended to mock
The ignorance of the damned who belittled him
Till a mockery mocked a mockery and we visited him.
Next shades of forgiveness pierced us from all directions,
And the sound of it was the silence of Bethlehem.

A Poem From the Woods

Little cottages were gathered together
Where the blue was crushed between them,
And the sky boy could not return there
To his mother who felt thick germs
Snapping in her hair like cat claws
That would rip the wood around the locks.
Like trees too sad and blue to talk,
The cottages were victims of this air
That finally wilted under the hush of night
And was found in the morning like saffron
Twisting in the hyde of a lonely bear.
There were yellow toes of an elephant near by
Where the tulip snow was more than shy,
And a magnolia tree was like Albert Einstein,
The magnolia of an ironing board dolphin
Where the woods still remained wrinkled.

The Diamond Sonnet

Compared to my love for you diamonds would blush
As they tremble in the twilight with the march of the dawn,
Smaller than this great silence that lives between us.
Roses walking naked, walking sideways through the seams
Of the moon, they would whisper a promise and be gone.
Back to the soul's window and your light song I move
Around those diamond facets that fail near your face,
And falling under the twinkle in your eye like a lake
{Proud green child that it is compared to this taste},
I taste the white pepper of your tongue and belong
To the scent of the years when your body was long.
Oh how long I have wandered here folding the deep,
Without end this length of days beyond the dew,
To find you in our home where the diamonds weep.

A Romantic Sonnet

When shadows were sweet to the touch no one noticed,
Where man and wife kissed in the lot.
Gentle hands were wet under their clothing
Where shy clouds drifted to the top,
Up the chimney of the moon where people
Cried later knowing they missed the fair scene.
Where all of the moons were moulded together,
They lit up the sky like one pretty white dream
On one pretty white day of invisible bliss
When the man was proud no one knew of this kiss.
When shadows were white to the touch they were tasted,
And such shadows were soft touching the tongue
That stood out over the echoing of waters,
And no one else walked on this shadow, no one.

Flowers Sometimes Lie

Someone told me you didn't love me anymore.
It was one of those flowers I bought at the store

Where I went shopping for your birthday in June.
Outside of the market he played the strange tune.

An ugly carnation was this horrible pink
I took out of the bouquet and left in the sink,

But no one believed him. My friends, they all sighed
And told me to tell you that flowers sometimes lie.

So I told you not to trust them, sweet words from their lips,
And to know that these flowers had very naughty hips.

They had loved one another, yes all at one time,
And this one who was jealous, I dyed him lime.

I told you that the dying of flowers must sting.
I remember you laughed then and said I must bring

Him out to the yard and we'd give him to King.
The others I taught to do nothing but sing.

$\mathcal{E}$lope

The plastic night was like a tape recorder
Keeping old songs that were written to elope
With himself, "staring Stanley" who was a narcissist,
And who wore an old black frown over his hope.

The police knew his little black was very lysergic,
So he told them what they wanted to hear
When they shouted that he was not this cold writer
Who held some strange twisted tree the most dear.

He watered the tree and told a psychologist
That when young he had swallowed his mind
About something he once read in the Bible
That said not to "cast pearls to swine."

With some reservation she helped him keep calm
Since sad Stanley loved staying that way.
He wanted to get over his social anxiety,
So he extracted a high place to pray.

He cursed in the temple and stood there lying
About why this mad Christ faced the cross.
He said that it was because life was a frown,
And so eternity was proud of the loss.

They found him dead with his tape recorder,
And the last little word on it was elope,
Making "staring Stanley" the new crown of thorns.
"Eloi, Eloi, lama sabachthani?" he spoke.

The Coward

One potato was strangely yellow with a green end,
And the other was too white like an elbow bone,
But the children thought it was pretty like a daisy
With a green eye and white leaves that had grown old.
It wasn't a young coward and so expected an excuse
For staying home from potato school until the noose
Was on its conscience nearly choking out the life
As it hung from my old tree, "a strange and bitter fruit."
I was startled when I saw it and knew why it did nothing.
It was just that the old coward couldn't face life anymore
Long before the little blond girl died in front of us all,
And I held her while the potato stretched out on its belly
Reminiscent of an old church bell that had fallen
Leaving an empty chamber above like a prison cell
Or hollow in a potato tree with a yellow smell.
My potato curved purple, very haggard and so disclosed
Of a pain that soared ever upward, taking off the nose,
{One of many longer eyes wearing the mask of Zorro.}
The mark of the coward lies in ignorance of sorrow.

The Right to Scream

Leaves bunch up like clouds in the sky,
Swaying on their blue trunks and branches.
All creatures hear the wind knocking on this wood,
Sometimes grayish with the tears of the moon,
And sometimes red when the sky is chopped,
Her artery round and blunted on the horizon.
This sky has unlimited veins like humans
And animals, and even complex insects
Who try to hide their rising and setting suns
From fear it will be found out that they deny time
Has any power over their sad inventions;
All failing to prove that death is an enemy
Who has no real right to scream in his wrath
That the echo is always louder than the axe.

Dangerous Well

Stratus clouds like starving women,
Well water splashes across the sky
Leaving us cold, and empty, and withered,
Trying to climb the sides of our cries.
Stones like bombs in a beehive cemented
Into our hearts that have hardened with war,
And yet we fear when the bombs are all shaved off
That no one will even care anymore.
Addiction to sorrow and pain and to nightmares
That warn us of how much death is to come,
Falling, and falling, and falling, and falling
Till exhale is all of our breath, and hope
Is nothing but valor since courage has wandered
Like a long thick tongue when silence spoke.

Smaller

Gentle bird of whispers whose promises are thin,
We are beings of shadow and are smaller than sin
So we let you have flat conversations with the wind.
Walls run out of words but words run out of walls.
There is nothing left but smaller till there is no more small.
Fine print exacted with a razor on the stone,
The clouds are like scratches on the sky, tiny bones
With their tiny blue sparks, mankind's dying call.
Silence in gray clouds grows dim till sound falls.
Through millions of dimensions a message is sent.
When stars pulsate with relief that their heat is all spent,
The poor all feel poorer and the darkness is bent
Like up ended nails that won't let the stars fall.
Walls run out of words but words run out of walls.

Owl's Dungeon

Wise men soar above a prison for lonely souls
Who could never make ends meet with the lines
Or keep the dense body of their wisdom fully attached
To those longer sentimentalities usually pressed
Against the heart as if it were the same essence
As a great owl's lungs anxiously filtering musky wind.
The horrors of the wise are wrapped in beauty
Dwelling with saddened children on a black cloud
Until night falls as it must into that dungeon
Of failure where the floor is covered with sunflower seeds
That all look like tiny owl's wings of inhuman need.
Tucked back behind their dungeon breast that is matter,
Owls fly with the names of the nameless and the dead,
Breaking the seeds of reincarnation in sacrifice to the gods.
It is death's hunger that lingers here at impossible odds.
Though owls fast forever, still death tends to eat
Considering the digestion of old white memories,
Since steel blue sky must always take the place
Of a dull white wrinkled rose,{the cerebral cortex}
Which is our complex reasoning ability
Surveyed by the limbic shadow that is love.
Men seek intuition that resembles an owl's beak
When they wait in this gray dungeon for old morning
Like one blue impenetrable sunflower seed high above.

Solomon's Cave

Darkness hardens in the mind being sucked
Against the walls of this cave by fishes
Attached to the outside like a tornado
Circling in confusion that is impenetrable.
The winds of the wise become petrified like stones
Imbedded in the walls of his cave with black bones
That are like veins of obsidian, the wise knowing sin;
And so morbidly they are acquainted with the sacred.
Here sits the breath of Solomon's heart beat
And the worship of these black angels of mercy
He finds hidden in each drop of the deep blue sea.
Gray conscience is swallowed by the hollow fear of God,
And so Solomon in his hard cave is permeated by beauty,
Black rubies like passionate roses throbbing sweetly.

The Smell of Bees

Once old sorrow has set it never moves
Like the hardened red sun sunken into grooves
Between the mountains or ripples of the sea
Resembling lilacs at night or the smell of bees.
The sun stings my face like little green nettles
That are the bitter failure of hearts of metal,
Such strange inverted gold, or silver, or steel
All stuck on their butts refusing to feel.
A heart should be more like a wet sponge
That takes in and lets out emotion like a tongue.
But once given too much and its root is pulled,
It runs out of its socket like a charging bull.
This night is all eaten and that old smell of bees
Is the same as lilacs that were smelled by knees.

The Sea and its Friends

High waves flutter like wings in the wet breeze
With the whole sky moving as it meets the sea.
Saturation worries where the water finds itself,
And sunken colors turn brown, bent into an elf
With purple fingers laughing and noses for toes
Or that breath of salt air when the satin wind blows.
The winter sea is feet and in summer is hands,
Long fingers with golden thumbs set in the sand.
Devotion rhymes with ocean when its sexy and deep
Like the belly of a wolf whose standing water is meat.
The sky's hunger never stops though the oceans collapse.
It seems endless, and deeper, and sharp as an axe
With tight introduction to the sea and its friends.
Like creatures of the sand, we are all made of ends.

What Happened to the Remote

A winding staircase sneezed near the top
Where one of the steps was cracked and fell through
While I was hurrying to escape a black cat,
Her disgusting tail and the mouse she kept batting,
How she frightened me with her high arching friendship
Held with a shadow that quickly grew

Into knowledge and wonder, though always blackened
By the sins of ambition which tried to have sex
With this troubled shadow, but settled for feeding
On the lies and forgiveness that came from its breast.
Only the shadow of this black cat was motherly
Because she herself cried to free a red wreck.

"Redwreck! Redwreck!" cried the staircase creaking,
Its claws red with blood from the tortured mouse;
But the reason it sneezed was because it was keeping
The tortured mouse close till the cat step fell through
Since to save this mouse's soul would be murder,
And with that the slick rails started sneezing too.

They sneezed on the gloves I wore for protection
To see if I might throw this black cat off
To its death far below on a bed of nails
That I saw long ago and never knew why
I stepped on them all before reaching the staircase
I near missed and then secretly wanted to die.

One hand on the staircase and holes in my feet,
I struggled to grip the other sneezing rail,
And when finally I did it my stomach was aching
So much that this strange ascent seemed to no avail.
I couldn't see the first sense in slowly growing old
Since this high top held nothing but my remote control.

It kept changing to channels that I never picked
When I finally got to the couch upstairs,
And my ankle was swollen where the cat had bitten
When she looked into my eyes with an evil stare.
I prayed for her shadow to reason with this enemy,
So that only the shadow would perch in my chair.

The Pink Pump

Disappointment is a wandering path at the joint
Of a crossroads beneath an outcropping of rocks
Where large sheets of shale hide the dark facts
And figures that made secrecy so necessary to me
Long ago after my worst mistakes were discovered
To have made life precarious if not oddly pernicious
Like the head of a wild black stallion disobedient
To even the most patient of trainers who forsook him.
I stood here with an arrow pointing to the sandy bed,
And that's when it all came to one dull red head.
We needed water so I found an old pink pump
At the end of this wandering path stuck beyond the dump.
I saw a sad tired friend leading my pernicious stallion,
Rope in one hand and in the other a rose sugar lump.

The Pink Cliff

A sheer pink cliff stood facing the ocean
Where rocks below bent, stained with gray emotion,
And that beard of steel shaved like the waves
With each hair was strong and incredibly brave.
At night the tide rose to challenge this pink razor
Where flowers buttoned to the neck amazed her.
The sunset regarded this cliff with full shape.
The moon drew waves back to dissolve them in place.
The sky rubbed hairs off but left stubble behind
To slowly swell up near the pink razor's mind.
Against this high cliff the cold ocean soaked
Into her breasts with dull curving of hope.
The nightingales whispered of colors unsung,
And so very plainly their countenance hung
Like tongues pressing gently an indigo light.
Sad songs held the doubtful tide against night.
Beneath pink and blue a shy purple dissolved
As the humming of sand, my sleepy silk wall.

Ocean of the Purple Heart

When I stare in a trance at the bleeding ocean
I wonder if I might read my books through the stains
That sprout the woody seeds of the hurt Nazarene
Nailed to a memory where emotion must remain.

A lot of pressure on the ears never to remember
Like two black deaths that sink into his eyes,
Right through the temples push the law and the prophets
Also trying harder to make his purple lungs divide.

Grape cluster lobes and the stem of medulla
Like the socket where a branch is connected to a tree,
Secret logic of the heavens in waves of gray bones
Must ache for holy darkness to cover his agony.

This medal breathing like one rainy old octopus,
Sad soldiers reach the shore with pink tentacles of hope
Common to many people who have never been in wars,
Their frayed cloth submerged, that could not marry but eloped.

Wooden cuts are stitched by purple medics who frown,
Using black threads like insects as all threads must be
With their tiny colors that seem to be electric,
Red sparks between the heavy magnets of the sea.

Purple Fairy

From black and blue warts a purple fairy was born
With green wings that could fly on cloud muscles.
He welcomed the rain and expected red stains
Since his eyes were them {red things, the scriptures.}

I noticed his rhyme, The Eunuch's Valentine
Caught admitting to painting blue pictures.
They put him in a jar, those marines he called scars,
Saying "You are me. I'm navel. I'm sick sir."

They paid no attention and left on vacation
So this fairy took to using red bottle brushes,
And washed the inside until he nearly died
When they found him in soap suds all blushes.

His muscles were weak but he came to a peak,
Soon was purple again and quite proudly
Unscrewed the lid with his black tongue that did
Turn those marines off to eating purple squid.

His wings were all right, and he flew then at night
To high green stars we elected as rangers.
His old motto last night had been never to fight.
His new motto was that rangers are never strangers.

The Inhuman Sea

This man of steel seems to weep with tears of night,
Drifting on a muscular tide out to the inhuman sea
Eventually gathering to fall off of the edge of the world
Where the universe becomes magnetic and collapses
Into this black rainbow garden where bent divinities
Are always kneeling in prayer for the children of men
Who are overwhelmed by my brave man's face of amen.

This man of steel has eaten seaweed so he weeps
These flattened tears of gold that are the keys to lofty gates
From suspicious heavens we are flown off to when we die,
The result of impossible expectations of an old blue future
Anxious to go and sit where the salty angels wait.
I call to them in this life where my nerves cross tired eyes
Since there is nothing as confusing as the music of the sea.

Here are the songs of all human sexuality long past
Into those most tightly abstract conceptions of eternity
Which have attracted inumerable minute sparkling suns
Like little silver fish rising to erase human consciousness
That has been crowded out by the feet of lost humanity,
Since after all our footprints are only our own reflections
At last leaving the summit of such improbable directions.

It is the cold inhumanity of it all that puzzles me
As I sit above on this cliff unable to traverse below,
Leaving those footprints unexplainable as little black paws
That disturb the sensible sand with their insubordinations,
Challenging the peaceful acceptance of all that must show
Whatever is hidden under green wings that turn to brown
When the cruel inhuman sea closes its purple mouth and frowns.

Images of Death

Pale passageways that lead above a mountain,
Subdued red lips of the sun which paralyze men,
The commands of a winter tree heard screaming,
Weightless formations of birds twisting upward
Until no more rays of the sun relocate their shadows;
Mourners walk only on the heaviest scent of the pines.
Imposters gather the broken arrows of our lungs
To the great weight of the rocks that seal everything
Without passing judgment on such impossibilities as life,
Since she has married this sudden stillness of sorrow
In the afterglow of two tears that became impassioned.
The tears of a thousand rivers stand out on our bodies.
The trembling of a million moths turns to sparrow feathers.
The terror of a fire reverses into the words of ashes.
Strangers meet the expectations of portrayed images,
And nothing hearts have not touched will survive this cliff
Where the purple breath of sad gods has somehow wandered
When a black sliver of time fell from their hollow tree;
And I myself never once realized there were so many of me
As the iron leaves of the deep of the mortuary sea.

A Story of Survival

Who ever thought that they might forget
What they saw in the evil September
When life was crowded out by a tragedy
Until only the old black wind agreed
On wiping off all of those maddening marks
That even gentle water wouldn't admit
Did not belong on my sandstone cliff.
It must have been myself behind this eggplant
That was the ocean I once crossed to survive.
Although now death seems so small in my hands,
There were still things her gray sky did not know,
Like the moon inside of my eggplant night
When all she wanted was for me to deride
This headless horseman with his ugly ridicule
That even abject souls would not admit
Did not belong on God's sandstone cliff.
My bucket and nothing to wipe with but fish,
I went to work with the moon in my grip,
Sponging off all of those salmon colored letters.
I wiped them right off like petals on my hip.

Daffodils

Daffodils will climb
Green stems in vase of water
Steadfast memory

Nothing's two faces
Must cancel out each other
Piece of wet paper

Afghanistan

The daffodils of my lonely nativity high on their
Maple dresser combed pennies of such dying hair
Into a knot on top of their pale Afghani heads.
Like some white fabric that had since yellowed,
They cast lots for the wilted ammunition of dresses.
Coming down white from the mountains into the woods,
They show us only one black muzzle with which to hurt
The trees with their green eyes of sympathetic moan,
For no one else would listen to their coats of death.
Women whose mouths were open from prostitution
In those poppy fields where all was sweet rest;
They left us faces fluted as illegal victims
Who would rather be hooded to innocence
Than to wind up reading yellow upside down.

The Queen's Regrets

A song of greensleeves affording to regret
With the sentiment of nobility, sad shoulders of a queen,
Her full gown as an apology all rumpled to gather
Her people who showed a purple mother must rather
Forgive as if her rich cake was the high father's wife
Who taught that God was nothing like the handle of a knife.
Regret as vanilla clams developing black pearls,
Strange carbon life forms as the smallest of worlds;
Lower chocolate was a magnet to specks of orange sand
That swelled up and worked out like a sliver in God's hand.
Marbled, a grape vine in lemon cake might echo
Under red fans in a face with the layers of a frown,
This cherub's brow now furrowed with a burnt umber brown
And mint designs like the broken tail of a gecko.

March of the Cows

One of those lazy days when cows moon in the sky
Remembering sheep and camels like a white disk,
A question mark lay face down in pajamas
Crawling through the third of March at full risk.

Three thousand three hundred and thirty three,
The exact date equals three pairs of cows on their knees,
Six threes face down like double humped camels,
The symbol of their offspring six, six, six for the beast.

Nostradamus was a prophet who saw a similar date,
Three thousand three hundred and ninety seven,
The world's end after a thousand years of peace
That might finally blow a wind back to heaven.

But three billion three hundred and thirty three,
{six zeros according to the book of William}
Brings astronomers who say that in four billion years
Our sun will swell up and peel earth like an onion.

A cow onion must be the reddish-purple kind
That gets madder and madder when it cries
Squealing like a cow-mouse from mouse-cow
Since the Vatican had once lost the authority to bow.

One priest was concerned about his milk pet,
Seeing how people said that animals are never heavenly.
But only the worst will be marked six, six, six,
And on the forehead of his cow, three, three, three.

Ancient Cameo

The heat that sears my expression passes
Like trees and their branches pass over shade,
And the sun crucifies such complexity
That sacred love rests with the night finally.
The thin hairs around your face are such bliss
That I would worship the dark word mankind
Because you are in it, an ancient cameo,
Something coming to me where I have died.
Time has died in every place where I stood still,
The boring trunks of trees without cool wind;
But now whipping through all forms I hear
A promise that love is the end of my sins.
Before I met you I could never move my legs
Or occupy old memory as hope turned in.

Remember the Rain

The fever of the light turns down,
And rain must fall to the earth
Where leaves are clear and lakes are green,
The slipping of the mud into man.
His blood of flowers is seldom seen,
About as often as love must kiss
Those yellow fears and yellow tears
That are on the endangered list.
The love of an enemy is very small
But more lives about the tear of a man.
It is the bullet that will strike a deer
Or a tongue of moss on the land,
Or a world all its own that never dies
Unless God eats the setting sun
Instead of hiding the night in his pocket,
Or that God would worship the lonely one.
There is no God who is not the powerful will,
The will to survive and hate and love.
But survival is stronger whenever the mind
Sees that fear only means the sun is late.
No talking, no laughter compared to this bliss,
Would I not choose because of night
Being what I remembered until the rain came,
And I knew that I had always been right.

Pretty Predictions

Before the show dancers powdered their faces
With pretty predictions that history would be met
Like a compact some beautiful old woman had left
In the subtle pink audience of Persephone's best.
High music suffusing the galleries, bending down,
Like plants that frowned with folded hands,
Her beauty too red for the church's pews;
The decaying greens from a distance grew
Infinitely cooler, stealing the soft melody
From the tips of her toes like a doll planted
In a clay pot that became the oval stage.
Yellow tea leaves passed by the couple unveiled.
Something was missing, his flat steps pale,
Without which, turning, her friends had bowed.
Fearfully handsome, they looked at his motive,
A man's chastity unheard of before the back
Was turned and death became his strong body.
Adding blue androginous sweet peas and climbing
Till the little black crosses lay down on her legs
In rows, her audience dead asleep, she frowned
Knowing her ballet would be called The Apocalypse.

Ruins of the Carousel

Awakened by the puckering sound of a carousel,
Children jump yellow ropes at dawn
Where cloud unicorns leap the highest hurdles.
Purple marks grow over the centuries
On pink walls of twigs that shake with the shadows
Of flared nostrils and turned heads.
Brown leaf horses drink from their own breasts
In their anger for misty rainbow pupils
Covered with the eclipses of moon stumps.
The horses have heavy metal storm hearts
To pursue black unicorns and their smaller infinity
Always turning on the outside edges of identity
Where broad green tongues protrude into the dusk,
And carousel personalities melt into the sea.

Flower Pies

Colorful flowers thick with the dew and sweet
Like sails on a boat where damp shadows meet,
Like a blanket that withers and floats and sighs,
The cool blue sun makes us flower pies.
What was that strange substance once called shy,
Green blankets in summer that never must die.
The sun is a yellow daisy baked in gray crust,
Love's morning that warms up thick angel dust
That settles on her rose pie like redwood men
Embarrassed by lilac ladies who whispered amen
Before they were taken like pink petals to church
Where intelligence told us there were many mirths.
The mirth pies like satyrs all tasted like wine
Of which the full moon in autumn leaves was lime.

A Portrait of Morning

Soft fingers of dawn massaged the cool air
Until slowly its warmth of movement returned,
And the morning secured by its breath rung out
With the proud sound of a shimmering bell.
Many birds circling in this opening rejoiced
Since they were able to follow an echoing light
That moved faster and faster until bliss appeared
With the brilliance of the sun that filled their ears.
Then deaf with delight they soared up to the clouds,
Meditation exacting the cumulous shapes
In formations of a mother to multiply the great
Silver blossoms that sprung from love's falling echo
With the blissful lips of a bell at its limitation
Like petaled mountains of morning speaking to the sun.

The Planet Tulip

Heavy fatty rain falls like clear lipstick
On these laughing phosphorescent people
Whose shiny muscles twist and wriggle
Like the red lipstick trees that vibrate
On this hilarious planet where all liquid
Is thick like a spongy banana smoothie.
They love to play with their long navels
That are supple and sexy and pink
And are used much on Tulip for kissing,
Or consulted by the masters who think
For hours about the forbidden sea-ming.

All of the carbon works its way into the ming,
Attracting people with its waves that sing.
This black sea has killed many couples
Who are drawn into it by its waves like hair
That are the only proteins living there.
They say the sea-ming holds the greatest passion
Away from the funny shimmering of the air;
But creatures who enter it die in a nightmare
About a world that is serious and actually solid,
Where they have something strange called unfair.
Some have ridden the singing waves back to shore,
Afraid of what weird earthlings call clothes
And the stretchy lipstick we call panty hose.

Heavy rain falls into Tulip's open faces
Which only close very tightly at night
When no one dares gaze at the violet sky
Lest they mock the masters who see it and cry,
Reading letters by lovers written in the sea-ming.
Isometric in their approach to obedience,
Tulips press hands on wet faces to pray
With deep expressions of clouds like flowers
Resembling colorful varieties of storm blocked suns
Which there are thirteen of for those loops
Stretching the ridiculous orbit of Tulip,
A bodybuilding planet where they eat mostly beets
And avocados in the waxy Tulip heat.
The food reaching their stomachs in fat feet,
They run to digest the breathing of the wheat.

Creation Myth

The taste of a lemon was bent on the tongue
Because nothing was better than water
That came from a mountain named after this one,
Like the sun that was thought of as a daughter.

The moon drank lemonade and puckered at night,
Feeling better about appearing at the dawn,
Since she was the mother of all of the living
And even dark space who got married to a lawn,

Green space or alternate space, the moon's sister,
So that this old moon had shot very fast
From dark elf space to green space and back again
Preparing for their wedding in the ancient past.

All the star sisters of the dark elf were straightened
So they no longer were up to such mischief
As supernovas and red giants and pretty dwarf stars,
When triple space came back with a great gift.

This gift was the worship of the father of creation
Who no longer would leave our moon mother alone.
He told a scary tale that our dark space was meat,
And of course that the moon was his bone.

Our moon mother bone was like a musical instrument
Resembling a very big white sand dollar flute,
And she plays now a melody for her husband triple space
About how now all three universes are cute.

87

The dark elf and green space gave birth to miles.
Before they traveled everything was quite close
Except for triple space who was very transcendental,
At last back from his silence and now sleeping the most.

The yawning of triple space seems to us to be angels,
Since they travel at the set speed of light.
But to children on earth they look just like lemons,
The juice of which has been made into kites.

Oh I've drunken kites and that's why I'm crazy
Enough to believe in some fat triple space,
And also mother moon, and her son who was lazy,
And green space like an object that is used to erase.

Buffalo

Existence resembles a herd of buffalo.
Every hump is a galaxy with a shaggy mane;
The utter universe a stampede over dry grass
As if the stars were all stretched out under
The pressure of time that is the weight of space,
Mostly dark matter eyes reach for most urgently
Like human finger tips groping at the senseless
Limits of perception where existence has fainted;
The thickness of the neutrality of consciousness
That is all pervading, overthrowing our balance.
The human navels are deep dark buffalos,
Our portals to the infinite parentage of life,
Receiving arrows of infinity that struck worship
Into our mundane hearts before we were primitive
As the promise of existence early hunters knew
Was sweet sorrow the night shared with us all,
The uttermost existence until reality sweated me.

Lonely Ocean

Why do rivers run into the open heart
But that the soul is a lonely ocean.
Its love breaks with a steady rhythm
Always repeating some tragedy past
Its senses then sleeping momentarily
On a foreign shore before being sucked
Out into an uncertain future deeper
Than sorrows could ever reach, cold
And numb with the perfection of silence.
Only this secret reality must obey
A fierce and constant persecution
By the sun warming its surface with lies
Eventually welcomed as proof of a hostile
Environment making the soul's ocean pray
To evaporate into the clouds completely,
So that then all of this divine water
Might fall on the empty basin below
And finally awaken its murdered body.
Resurrection settles on the surface of everything,
On the ocean as nine billion black seagulls.

Pendulums

Golden death is rising simply in the sky
Above pointed trees that seem to cry
From purple wars narrowed with tears
That have yellowed behind old winter years.
I break the fat twigs, red figs of fears,
Deaf ears, sheep shears, strange winter gears
To find the moon sleeping on the ground,
Then in a boat push her out to sea.
The fever, the fever, the fever is me.
To slit the throat of world war is weird.
Leaves break the bottle and draw him near.
His pendulum swings inside the sun,
But the moon is a paper doll full of holes,
And her pendulum swings out into the cold.

Irons

Flower petals with their whittled smiles,
Unfinished children with shoestring eyes,
Words misquoted like green irons understood;
Water falls gently on old rocks of wood.

Pressing engagements with irons that sing,
Wax that never touches anything,
Fingerprints like apple blossoms on doors
That always turn black when the ocean roars;

The moon in a black laundry basket of night
Is flattened when finally sprayed with orange light.
The orange is a rhinoceros as all things must be,
Mist that dyes purple the highest peak.

A kiss was so rhinoceros nothing could move,
Erotic wax steam that flatened word rooms
Under this gray iron that sat like a storm
Or blue rhinoceros coat that seemed very warm.

He Was Different

Wild children have played in the rain but he was different.
His mother called him but little Michael ignored her.
Her decided his old puddle would do nothing but bore her.
Michael's myrtle was more than mother's dark heart had seen,
So he reached out and affectioned this puddle of green.
With his ear to it he listened since it had been silent
As if the patient rain also had fallen in slow motion,
And he saw in this his future in modern science,
Thinking, though impossible, mirrors would be made of water.
Michael wondered why in his puddle he always spoke in French,
So he slipped in for supper muttering nonsense,
Then laughed and told his mother he learned the word dense.
Nerdlihc tsom naht retrams gnikool mih demialcorp elpoep.
In the morning he snuck out and put his puddle in a bottle.

In Memory of Jalopy

A jalopy of grapes hung over his head
Where cumulus clouds were imposing
Their threats that alcoholic rain must fall
As soon as Anonymous our cat left the meeting.

Anonymous was a handsome black specimen
Who mourned for his calico bride named Jalopy,
Since she had died from being given only beer
By someone who thought that sobriety was weird.

There was a man who fancied that he was anonymous
Since he and his friends never admitted their crimes,
And they all went to his wedding to a black girl
Who was rich enough to clean the toilet with wine.

Anonymous found his way to the criminal's house
Where he was proud that he caught the man's mouse;
But when the man tried to give Anonymous beer,
The black cat spoke this, "I am better than weird."

The criminal then bought a terrier named Weird
And gave the poor dog beer to drink too;
But Weird ran away and barked at a cop,
Then spoke these words, "I'm Weird and I'm blue."

Rattler's

An old glass rattle is rippled and dim
Like sunlight made of nylon vomit to speak
That if men are whiskey, then women must be beer,
And the rattles on the sides of their heads are weak.

Ear Beer is Near Beer since it listens to sober
Heads that get soggy just sitting in Alvin Fake
Waiting for whiskey to ferment in a graveyard
Where long ago they buried professor Edmund Snake.

The grass there was whiskey and often brown
In November when a rattle could always be heard
In the voices of mourners who gathered at noon
When whiskey was freely given to hurt nerds.

They wore strange green boots with jangling spurs
That were used on a horse named Whiskey whose tail
Was always jealous of his mane we found fastened
At the stern of a boat to a rattlesnake sail.

This horse tried to hold back the wind as it billowed
In a sail that was every bit as lovely as glass,
Since some said that Rattlesnake Whiskey was Satan
Who slept on the surface of the ocean at black mass.

About the Bitter Truth

Shy ladies don't lie, they only silently swear
That weird lacy stockings are the proper sizes
When sad grandmother wraps them for Christmas,
And they feel her soft black cheek as they kiss.
A bind lady would exchange them at Pennys and wear
Disfigured stockings sitting down with grandmother
At tea in early March when there was still snow,
Since feelings would be exactly multiple
Instead of thrown aside rumpled on a chair
Where patterned green stockings crush tiny red blades.
Oh what sense has the bitter truth ever made,
Set like millions of sixteenth inch Christmas trees
When a black star of cruelty made honesty a disease?
{The dark secret kept under blue satin slip covers.}

A Late Valentine

I'm writing a blue valentine to sit beside the pink,
And now that we're getting older, soon too old to think,

We will be getting wrinkled like the sky before a storm
When the ironed sun is setting, and blankets keep us warm.

It's late, almost the end of February facing March,
And I'm remembering a kneaded eraser rubbing art.

It could have been silly putty since a valentine is that,
Pressed against cartoons and picking up their rats.

A rat is an apartment where an oldster's shadow sits
And plays with cats because he's a man who knits.

So knitting a blue sky with poetry of brackish yarn,
These words in rows are as wet as fertilized farms.

My valentine farm has blue water running in rows,
But instead of food what sprouts up are pretty bows.

I put one on my valentine to prove how storms are striped.
Gray clouds are cats of thunder, the tinted blueish type.

A steel cat is full of oxygen that plays with Rusty's ears.
I'll be adopting it when he dies, when it's full of tears.

Reunited

Mister Peabody was a very clever man,
A gentleman in every sense of the word
Except for his huge overgrown appetite.
He spent his grants largely on meat and wine.
Mister Peabody was quite popular at school
And soon acquired a position mitigating letters.
It started as soon as the little yellow cap came up,
And he worked hard every day until the dark
Diet Pepsi Mountains gave sparkling information,
And those liquid birds were most refreshing.
He was in his Bently when an alien called
Mister Peabody on the company car phone.
He was directed to drive straight to the ocean
Where he saw the fantastic creature come up.
It was all a lovely pink and looked exactly
Like his pretty ex-girlfriend assuming that she
Was somehow pregnant from four different wombs.
Mister Peabody did the only right thing.
Exposing his huge unattractive awkward body,
He swam into the water and loved the creature
Until there was nothing left of his mind.
He was famous thereafter for the strange day
The fat ocean turned to green alien wine.

Father Forgive Them

Mankind is insane since leaving the innocent stream
Born to Eden where the berry bushes are a dream.
Dreams of God are chaos since we know not what we do,
And scientists say that automatic reaction is their school.
Reaction is a ridiculous echo adopted by this world
Where Jesus taught we were seeds like little babies curled.
Some claim it was bad karma, his humble manger scene,
Though this is what it meant to prove that love is not a dream;
That miracles of life exist and all must have their chance
To inherit love eternal from his precious glance.
If for the slightest instant you could see the face of Christ,
Do you think you would never know to offer sacrifice?
With saddened hearts "forgive them for they know not what they do."
There are many faces in the sacred night supporting me and you.

Pencil Box

My blue cardboard box meant for shoes,
The violet top was used as a sand shovel.
An empty envelope was glued to the back.
On the front where flowers once hoveled
Were directions to look to the sides
Which proposed never to send us the contents.

I'm sorry, I'm sorry, I'm sorry,
I'm sorry, I'm sorry, I'm sorry,
I'm sorry, I'm sorry, I'm sorry.

I'm sorry, I'm sorry, I'm sorry,
I'm sorry, I'm sorry, I'm sorry,
I'm sorry, I'm sorry, I'm sorry.

I'm sorry, I'm sorry, I'm sorry,
I'm sorry, I'm sorry, I'm sorry,
I'm sorry, I'm sorry, I'm sorry.

I'm nothing but twenty seven pink erasers
Like noses on the tops of forest green pencils.
On the bottom in yellow paint it reads THE END.

Black Worms

My ugly dog walked backwards and sat.
They called it God. It swallowed a cat
Who was the night, who scratched the moon
That really was a child of the womb;

That really was hair, that really was sweat,
That really was cloud, that really was net.
I screamed when this was my lonely birth,
Third worm from the sun, late planet earth.

Nobody respected but I didn't know
Was what they believed so forbid it to show.
Forbidness I thought of it as and so cried
All of those little worms who never died.

They loved them again when they were found
Juicy to eat and that made a strange sound.
Whoops! Later my dog wound up at the pound,
Third worm from the sun on planet Mounds.

Oh I was a nigger, a black worm a soul
Who looked something like wild rice in a bowl.
I screamed when this was my lonely birth,
Third worm from the sun, late planet earth.

Happy Mule Shit

It's no wonder women wash clothes under yellow shit
When people are sweating and smell bad from despair.
A welcoming mountain is stained by the distance
It has kept away from the stuffy morning.
The masters used to worship cleansing old vomit,
The vomit of the sun, the vomit of the moon,
And never speak but only squeak out the night.
Since tadpoles are unfriendly way up there,
They are lost on the wind with feet small as a wife.
We have transpositioned the wind hoping for darkness,
The void of sleep for the men and tired animals
Who climbed this mountain before and rested in the deep
Sdrawkcab deklaw yeht nehw oga gnol,
Amazed by the happy black. It was the mule shit!

Sue Shoe

She petitioned the dusty old mountains,
Red like a Merriam Webster Dictionary,
Soliciting the peaks against a master named Shoe.
He had claimed she was his common law wife
Who cheated on him, so she tried to sue,
{Drunken muddy cloud that she still was},
Calling it a case of slander in loose pants.
It was true that she got drunk with another man,
And Shoe plead they had sex against the mountain.
Considering he owned the place and knew his way,
There were three sets of footprints there
She called love's calligraphy of a family;
But Shoe proved she was living with him too.
All she owned in common law for six years,
He had kept and held dear with Shoe tears.
The third party was a servant he hated to pay,
Who used to groom his horses for a high wage.
She could not sue Shoe for lack of her dignity
Since the horses were limping about the screw,
And all of Shoe's true friends shouted boo!
It was obvious as shoe polish what master Shoe knew.

Complex Blueprint

Wet black trees of November crisscross the sky,
Disobedient to the lattices, forming their own shapes.
They speak of the ignorance of men and women
Who worry about the innocence of their own little twigs,
Disconnected, as humanity is, from the source of things
Like that complex blueprint behind the storms of reality.
Blue mercy is not one to wish for the pain of creatures
Who tangle from their fears of hell and destruction,
Twisted and horrified of death, that natural change
Merely switching from one branch to another in the wind.
On this spiritual tree three hands are found clapping
When at all distances meeting one hand finds us napping
And remembers that fifteen is the number for infinity.
Life is like a puzzle with fifteen hundred pieces,
Success being dependant on a clear picture of the divine
With its many eyes pressing in one thick hand,
The ancient past and future meeting with the present.
The proud and timeless eyes in this hand always vibrate,
But shyly I behold the eyes of humanity being bent;
And that I tried to find God in all things completely,
But laughed having learned only God could find me
Swimming in this blueprint that is the old blue sea
Where one hand clapping is the sound of eternity.
Why do I say that the divine I.Q. is thirty thousand
And pray I will not fall through God's eyes into despair
Where his fifteen hundred fingers would weep for me?

Wet Little Cries

Fields of wheat gather like children crying.
They are trying to escape from the wet ground
Where the wind hunts them like a wild boar,
The storm striking too low abnormally
Pushing the mud into piles around their stalks.
I had never heard it before but now the war talks,
Telling all of the secrets of lovers to the rain.
I scream that I am not a lover, so leave me alone!
I think I may escape into the trembling sky
And hold up the children, my arm full of cries.
I must not ever lose one, perishing below.
These ridiculous clouds have never even known
Not to give their rain to such a monsterous wind,
And now the mindless clouds are hunting me.
Like a priest they want me to hear their sin.
The clouds are hunting me! The clouds are hunting me!
And wet little cries dig under my skin.
They are the children of innocence who bore no sin.
I need them to take all of my soul's blood and fly.
I am the only one who knew their souls might die,
Their cries now the shrill screams of freedom.

The Lighthouse

I bought a bag of wheat called The Family.
There stood an angel looking like a white beard.
My son bought a bag of chaff and burned it,
And the name on that bag was Weird.

The Family had a picture on the back{of Mt. Rushmore},
But Weird showed a lighthouse by the sea.
My daughter took a bag of brown rice with pigeons,
And they flew in all the windows and ate me.

With Stones

Light moves upward
Winged universe rising
Planets of goose down

Where a fawn once bled
People left the river
With stones in sheets

The soldier's helmet
Echoed like two sparrows
In one drop of water

Under stormy skies
Mothers held their own hair
Without their sons

Match Book Lovers

Salmon is a collar blue
Niggers would strike unde covers.
Caraway, an open gate,
A day like that is for lovers.
Rushing by the blushing moon,
Their pansy beard eyed sailor
Combed them through the deeper blue.
A salmon bit the tailor.
The tailor god who never bled
But stitched his quiet wonder,
Found that in the black of night
His soul began to wander.

The White Pumpkin

There was a white pumpkin by the name of Avalanche.
People never carved it since it was full of black ants
That consisted of the halloween night, black pumpkin flesh,
And souls reincarnated from a sagging gargoyle net.
Friends with the white cactus, its skin grew horrified
That its white shell in its seedhood, people might pry.
Concerned, the master vegetable expected it to die
When the sun pumpkin saw this and sent down red lies.
Red ants swarmed everywhere electrocuting crops,
And the cloud ears all turned blue becoming many cops;
But the white pumpkin floated down, and some called it God
Who taught that the meaning of life was to be like Mrs. Odd.
This Mrs. Odd taught mercy in which a candle glowed
Under white grass of forgiveness, a glitter closely mowed.

The Cantaloupe Mountains

Sand like blond hair with long lingering trails
That have become matted where they crossed
Like rain that fell across a sunbathed sky
That was afraid to be gray, not wanting to die,
An axe fell like lightning revealing orange rock
That resembled fat cattle who all seemed to talk.
This cowboy who lowered it into the carrotwood
Thought that trees and green plants weren't for living,
And so he cut and ate up as many as he could,
And felt shy about Christmas, Jesus, and giving.
But the Cantaloupe Mountains were so saturated with sun
That this cowboy was warmed by their golden horses,
And got sunburned by the hyde of one appaloosa,
Then decided to elope with a little blond christian.

The Wet Mountains

Fold the stars into my waiting breast of night.
Lumpy shadows unwrap the morning with your smile.
Human breasts are the people of the Wet Mountains,
And their nipples are the distant trees.

Rain falls upward into the gravitational field
Until clouds creep back down into the night
Where they knit together like a granite tweed
That is the nuptial beauty of your wet skin.

I take your skin from the laundry, wrinkled and damp,
And cover myself with your red nipples too
When the trees are blushing with excitement,
So many Xs that turn distant trees to blue.

Sacred Little Girls

Blue and green sting each other describing the distant
Moment reluctant trees duck into the summer skies.
There are many faces to the blue and all of them are sacred.
They make me afraid I will no longer tremble here
With sacred little girls whose backs are so straight
That they hold restless birds to their penmanship.
Waring people, murmuring with activity, bright
Perfumed indian blossoms are nothing but sound
Vibrations, sweet wavelengths rather like blown glass
Causing silently angry multiple purple oceans to hang
Like a fushia the temperature of a baby's lips,
The red kisses our American Revolution sadly missed.
When hand made arrows were set hard against little red backs,
There were never any wars like those of the human beings.

Symphonic Red

The screaming of the universe, veins under the ground
And water soaking into the spiritual sky,
The small black faces of wild birds were drowned
In oceans of blood because God had died.
Then the wind started whispering, "time is paralyzed."
The white hairs of the wise left their dead heads
And were growing out of reddish-purple beets.
The war left fear in our veins where love walked,
And nothing was as blue as the blue of the poets in the street.
What the universe screamed, they deciphered it there
And grew it all back from the wells of despair.
Our conscience was baked like mother's breasts in the heat,
And nothing was as red as the symphonic red
Of the sweet little children long lost in the street.

The End of Nature

Men had sex with the trees in hate of their women.
Underhanded, turned down like painful moonlight,
Nothing left, more than hardened into sorrow,
When nature ended we looked for them on the rails.
The branches of tigers and the knot holes of bears,
The sound of ponds boiling wider than blindness,
Squeezing out from under them, souls tied to broken arms,
The insistence on breaking the sticks into the sky,
They spoke the word sacrilege, smaller, louder, threatening one
Who watched them, another seeing himself striking into place!
The screams themselves running faster than black distances,
No more death except for dying increasing its focal points.
When would it end but that means were the ends of hysterical
Inanimate consciousness searching hot pain for the first time?
Questions broke open, bending backwards, returning in fear.
Paralysis of hope, stars devoured the ground and disappeared
Then reappeared black, too tiny to make infinitesimal night
Stop concentrating on escaping from the increasing volume.
Squealing, the hyperventilating wind took over anti-time,
Releasing black flames, the burnt fish of vertical oceans.
Reality was torn! Returning was exiled! Everything shook!
This was the end of nature when the wind was all hooks.
This was the end of nature when men were dissolved,
And red monks looked for all that was left, the cause.

Printed in the United States
By Bookmasters